MW00950314

THE BIG
ADVENTURES
OF
LITTLE DUDE

"Little Dude and The Under the Sea"

By Stink Menges

Illustrations by Matt Shepherd

Copyright © 2021 Christina Menges

Published by CaryPress International Books
www.CaryPress.com

All rights reserved. No part of this publication may be reproduced, distributed, or transmitted
in any form or by any means, including photocopying, recording, or other electronic or mechanical
methods, without the prior written permission of the publisher, except in the case of brief quotations
embodied in critical reviews and certain other noncommercial uses permitted by copyright law.

XOXO
STINK
MENGES

This is Little Dude....

Little Dude's favorite things in the world are his adventures in the Under-the-Sea and his friends who live there.

His favorite place in the Under-the-Sea is in his very own clam shell. He's filled it with some of his favorite things:

His favorite toy: a **small tire** that he
found at the bottom
of the Under-the-Sea,

A **bowl of gravy**, his most
favorite treat in all the world,

A **cozy pillow** to snuggle upon,

And his picture of **Mother.**

His most favorite person in all the world is **Mother.**

Hello there!

Mother gives Little Dude hugs and kisses to remind him how much she loves him.

Every day, Little Dude looks forward to having lunch in his clam shell house with Mother.

She brings Little Dude his lunch every day, paddling out to the Under-the-Sea in her giant pumpkin boat.

Together they sit in Little Dude's clam shell house and have lunch while Little Dude tells Mother of his adventures in the Under-the-Sea.

One day, Little Dude asked Mother to join him for a walk in the Under-the-Sea.

Little Dude loved his walks in the Under-the-Sea. All of his sea creature friends would come out to say hello to him.

Today was a special day, though because today, Little Dude was going to introduce Mother to his Under-the-Sea friends!

As he and Mother walked along greeting all of the wonderful creatures living around Little Dude's clam shell, he beamed with excitement!

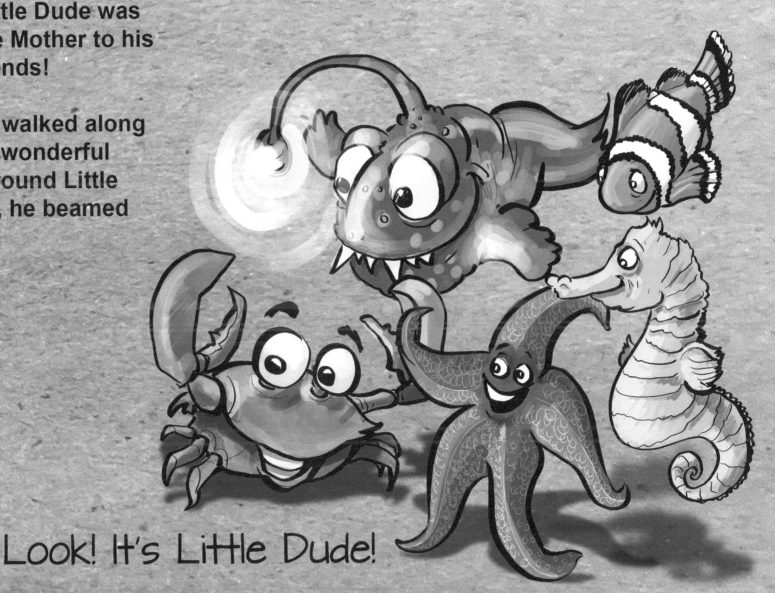

Look! It's Little Dude!

Soon they arrived at the large Conch Shell house.

This is where Little Dude's best friend, **Lincoln**, lived.

Lincoln loved to work in his garden making sand castles and growing sea weed to munch on.

"What a beautiful garden!"
Mother said.

"It looks just like the one I passed
on my way to bring Little Dude his
lunch! Only this garden was covered
in beautiful coral reef and had
hundreds of shells covering it! Do
either of you know who lives there?
It was so pretty!"

"Oh, that's Ferdinand's house - we
never go anywhere near his house!
No one likes him!
It's far too dangerous!"
exclaimed Lincoln.

"Why doesn't anyone like him and why do you think it's dangerous?" asked Little Dude.

"Well," Lincoln replied, "Ferdinand is as big as you can imagine! And he has thousands of long arms that he uses to grab the Under-the-Sea creatures when they aren't paying attention! Then he bites them into a million pieces with his sharp beak before he gobbles you up!"

"Oh no!" cried Little Dude.

"Oh yes," replied Lincoln.
"He's a terrible creature with large black eyes and enormous teeth! He's mean and horrible and ugly! He eats the Under-the-Sea creatures like you and me for his dinner every night! I even heard he just ate a poor little dog fish the other day who was just passing by his coral reef!

The dog fish hasn't been seen swimming in the Under-the-Sea since!"

"A dog fish!" cried Little Dude. "Why would anyone eat a dog fish, Mother?"

"I'm not sure, Little Dude, but I don't want you going ANYWHERE near that coral reef. It might be dangerous, as Lincoln said, and I don't want you to be eaten by any creature in the Under-the-Sea!"

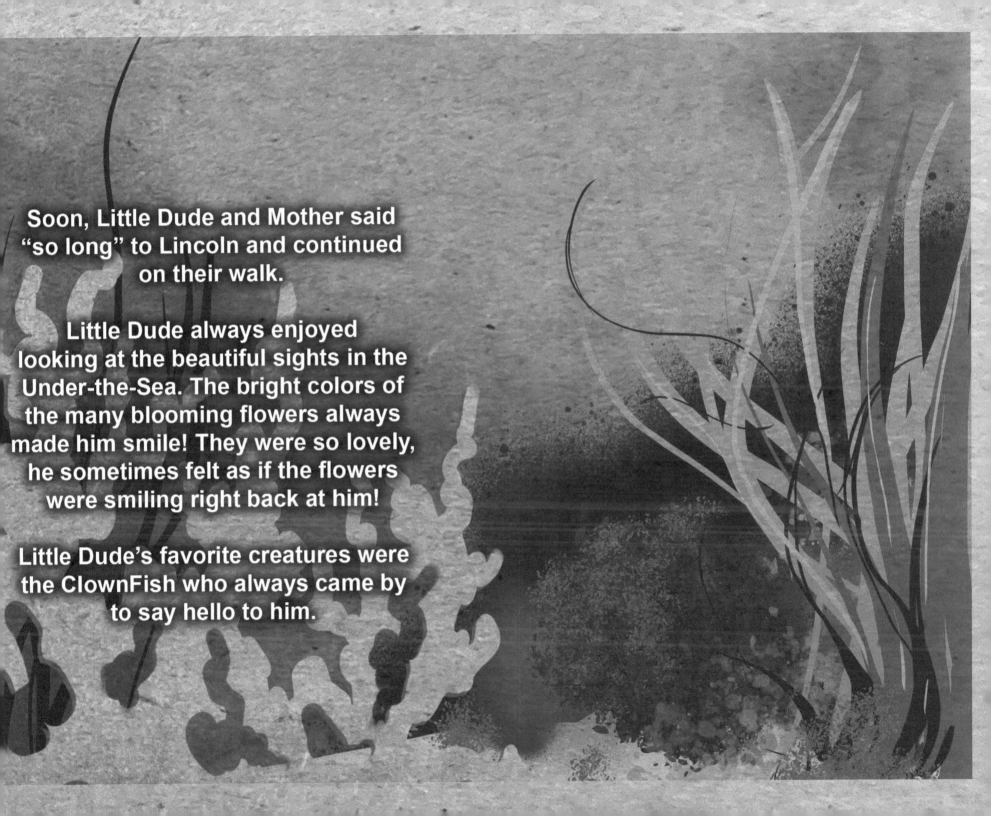

Soon, Little Dude and Mother said "so long" to Lincoln and continued on their walk.

Little Dude always enjoyed looking at the beautiful sights in the Under-the-Sea. The bright colors of the many blooming flowers always made him smile! They were so lovely, he sometimes felt as if the flowers were smiling right back at him!

Little Dude's favorite creatures were the ClownFish who always came by to say hello to him.

The Clown Fish and other Under-the-Sea creatures loved to do tricks for Little Dude: Back flips and twists and twirls and coils and spirals and loops and whirls!

Little Dude tried some back flips, too. Mother and the Clown Fish laughed and clapped and cheered him on, even though he didn't quite make it all the way over and fell onto his belly. But it was important that he tried and just had fun with his friends.

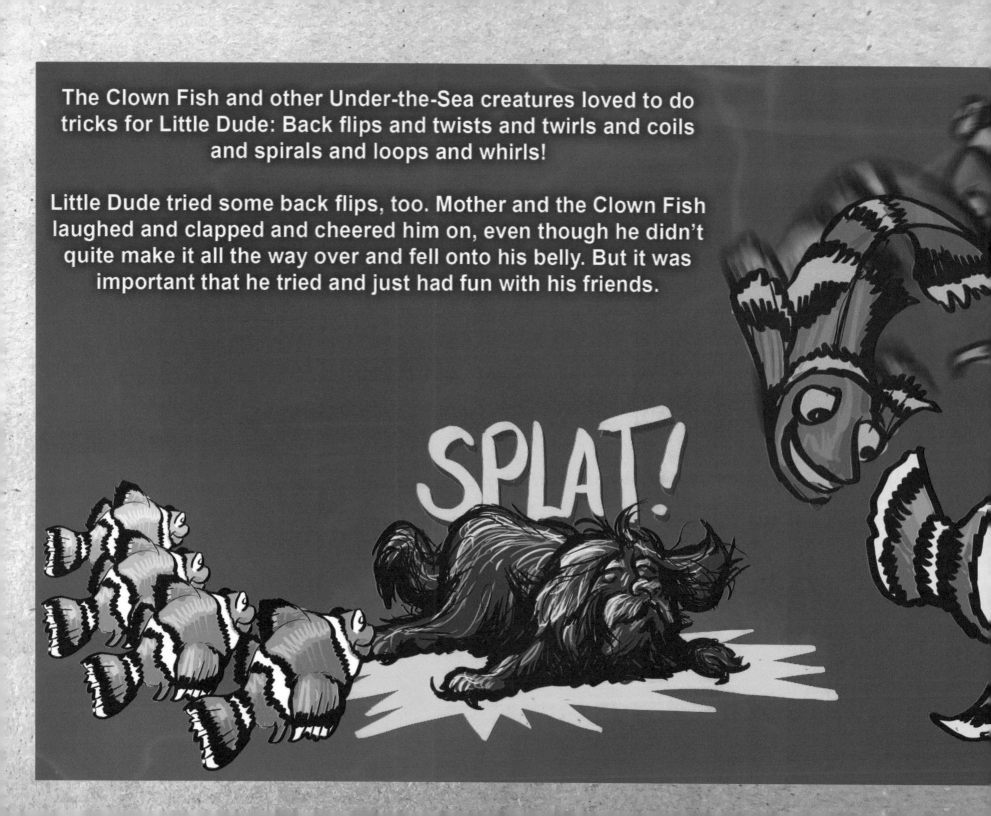

"Don't worry, Little Dude! We Clown Fish are born to do tricks and practice hard every day! If you practice, you might learn to do a back flip just as well as we do!"

The Clown Fish made Little Dude
feel better that he wasn't able to do a
back flip very well.

He and Mother promised to come
back and see them soon and he
would certainly have learned a back
flip by then!

As Little Dude and Mother continued on their walk waving hello to all of the Under-the-Sea creatures, they wondered at the beauty of the Under-the-Sea.

Flowers of all shapes and sizes and colors – some that looked like flowers, but were actually alive and waved their beautiful tentacles at Little Dude.

These were called Sea Anemone and were some of Little Dudes favorite sea creatures - not just because they were beautiful, but because they helped care for the entire sea floor and coral reef that he loved so dearly.

In fact, they were so mesmerized by the beauty around them, they didn't notice that they had walked right into the large coral reef that Lincoln had warned them about –

THE CORAL REEF BELONGING TO FERDINAND, the sea creature who had eaten the dog fish!

"OH NO!" cried Little Dude,

"It's Ferdinand's house! Now what do we do, Mother!"

Mother simply smiled and said, *"Not to worry, my darling Little Dude. If we don't bother him, he has no reason to bother us. Let's just continue on our walk and be on our way."*

As Little Dude and Mother continued on their walk, they felt something strange lurking behind them.

Suddenly, Ferdinand appeared! He was just as Lincoln had described! He was very large and very red and had long scary tentacles.

He had an enormous mouth with a massive beak that frightened Little Dude so much that he jumped into Mother's arms.

"Now don't be afraid, Little Dude," Mother said gently.

"Remember, if he we don't bother him, he has no reason to bother us. Let's just continue on our walk."

"You see, the little dog fish – his name is Harvey – is my friend who lives with me. He was lost one day a while back, so I took him in and gave him a home. I'm very worried that he might be lost in this big world in the Under-the-Sea."

"Oh my, that's terrible!" Mother said. "I don't know what I'd do if I lost my Little Dude! You must be so worried!"

"I certainly am," Ferdinand sadly replied.

"He's just a tiny little fish who doesn't know the dangers in the Under-the-Sea. I do hope that he isn't hurt. He must be so terribly frightened and feeling so all alone!"

A tear suddenly rolled down Ferdinand's cheek. He looked so upset and so sad that Little Dude felt sorry for him. He realized that Ferdinand was not a terrible sea creature at all and that he had misjudged him because of what he and the other sea creatures were told.

Mother then whispered to Little Dude, "Little one, why don't you try saying hello to this nice sea creature. He seems like he could be a new friend!"

Little Dude jumped down from Mother's arms and slowly walked over to Ferdinand.

He was still a bit frightened of the large creature about whom he had heard so many terrible things from Lincoln, but he couldn't help but feel bad for Ferdinand so he took a chance that he wouldn't be eaten by him.

"We can help you look for him!"
Little Dude kindly said
to Ferdinand.

"Oh! Would you!"
Ferdinand cried,
"I know everyone is afraid
of me because they
think I'll eat them,
but I'm actually quite nice.
I don't have very many
friends and Harvey is
my only companion.
I don't know what I would
do if he were lost."

"My name is Little Dude and this is my favorite person in the whole world, Mother!

She's very kind and will help us look for Harvey, won't you, Mother?"

"Of course, I will!" Mother replied.

"My name is Ferdinand and I'm pleased to meet you both."

Little Dude, Mother and Ferdinand looked for Harvey everywhere they could think of. From the bed of clam shells where the hermit crabs lived all the way to the grassy orchard of sea weed where the smallest creatures made their home.

Along the way, they ran into the friends of Little Dude and introduced their new friend, Ferdinand.

At first, some of the creatures from the Under-the-Sea were frightened, just as Little Dude had been, and hid themselves from Ferdinand.

But Little Dude assured them all that Ferdinand was kind and hadn't actually eaten the dog fish. He explained that Harvey was Ferdinand's companion and dear friend to whom he gave a home.

Soon, all of the creatures from the Under-the-Sea were helping in the search for Harvey.

As Little Dude searched, he sniffed his way along the sea floor and bumped noses with a sea creature he hadn't seen before sleeping under the empty shell of a horseshoe crab! The little creature awoke and,
although he was startled to see the little fish, Little Dude simply said,

"Hello there! Are you Harvey?"

"How did you know that?"
the little fish replied.

"Your friend Ferdinand has been looking for you! He's been very worried that you were lost."

"I did get lost," Harvey replied, *"but I got so sleepy trying to find my way home, I had to take a nap under this horseshoe crab shell."*

"Follow me," Little Dude said to Harvey, *"and I'll take you to Ferdinand! He'll be so happy to see you!"*

Harvey followed Little Dude to where Ferdinand and Mother and the other Under-the-Sea creatures were searching. When Ferdinand saw them, he cried,

"Harvey! I've been so worried about you!"

Harvey sprang into the many long and loving arms that Ferdinand tenderly wrapped around him.

"Thank you for finding my friend, Little Dude", Ferdinand said.

Once all of the Under-the-Sea creatures saw that Ferdinand was so happy to have found Harvey – and didn't actually eat him – they realized that they had misjudged him.

He wasn't a scary, terrible, frightening creature in the Under-the-Sea, but a loving companion who cared for Harvey.

They all understood that Ferdinand was someone with whom they could become friends and never have to fear again.

It wasn't long before Ferdinand and Harvey did become good friends with all of the Under-the-Sea creatures. Sometimes, they even joined Mother and Little Dude for lunch in Little Dude's clam shell.

Little Dude looked up at Mother as he watched Harvey and Ferdinand playing with all of the creatures in the Under-the-Sea.

"I'm so happy that we met Ferdinand and Harvey and became friends with them, Mother."

"I am too, my darling Little Dude.
Just remember:

We should never judge others by
what everyone has to say about
them. Use your own little nose to find
out what the Under-the-Sea creatures
are like.

They might just surprise you and
become lifelong companions like
Ferdinand and Harvey!"

About the Author:

Stink Menges began his writing career inspired by the songs that his father lovingly composed based on the experiences that they had together during their walks in the woods while camping, on the beach or just in their backyard at their home in North Carolina. He was adopted by his parents, Christina and Ashley Menges in 2012, when he was just 5 weeks old. Christina found him on the side of a road in the dead of winter and brought him to their home - then in Ohio - where he was welcomed by his brothers, Caleb and Trout. Today, Stink spends his time playing with his siblings Lincoln and Daisy-Bird Menges, camping in the mountains or on the beaches of North Carolina with his family - his ever-present tire toy at his side - enjoying his always-favorite bowl of gravy and continuing to write his stories for children around the world to enjoy!

CPSIA information can be obtained
at www.ICGtesting.com
Printed in the USA
BVHW090721230222
629819BV00001B/1